SUNSET IN PROVENCE

A TALE OF THE ALBIGENSES

DEBORAH ALCOCK

SUNSET IN PROVENCE

A TALE OF THE ALBIGENSES

cántaro
publications

cántaro
publications

www.cantaroinstitute.org

Sunset in Provence, Deborah Alcock

Published by Cántaro Publications, a publishing imprint of Cántaro Institute, Jordan Station, ON. L0R 1S0, Canada

© 2022 by Cántaro Institute. All rights reserved. Except for brief quotations in critical publications or reviews, no part of this book may be reproduced in any manner without prior written consent from the publishers.

Book Design: Steven R. Martins

Library & Archives Canada
ISBN 978-1-990771-19-4

Table of Contents

I

The Two Paths

"I'll never do it, never!"

The breath of these proud words seemed to thrill the banners that hung around the baronial hall of the Count of Toulouse. What was it the young Raymond Roger, Viscount Beziers, declared he would never do, as he stood confronting, almost defying, the powerful head of his house?

"My lord and my uncle may command my service in any lawful war, and my obedience so far as honour and conscience permit."

The old man interrupted him with an angry gesture. "Have the Counts of Toulouse ever asked anything of their vassals contrary to honour or conscience?"

"My lord, I am your sister's son but not your vassal," the youth replied with perhaps unnecessary pride. "But that is not the question," he added sadly and in a gentler tone. "You counsel me – no, you *command* me," and he bowed his head slightly the word, "to submit myself unreservedly to our Holy Father the Pope, in the person of his Legate."

"I do, as you do value life and lands. If your retainers had not infected you with their heresy, why should you hesitate?"

"I – the son of Roger Taillefer – a heretic! None of our race were ever that, thank Heaven.

But can the Count ask why I hesitate? Not that I fear the disgrace of a public penance, though I think they might have spared it to the greatest seigneur who speaks the 'Langue d'Oc', and altogether such a submissive and obedient Roman Catholic."

The Count's eye fell, and a flush of shame and indignation crossed his face.

"Do you taunt me with that?" he exclaimed. Then, with an effort, he cleared his brow, and, shrugging his shoulders, said in a tone of studied carelessness, "A knight might spend his days more joyfully in his lady's bower, or on his good steed following the chase, than kneeling at the tomb of some saint of very doubtful repute, with a scoundrel of a monk standing over him, scourge in hand. But, Nephew, your hands are pure from the blood of legate or churchman, and for the rest, you can plead youth and inexperience.

Draw on your treasury freely, bribe everyone, from my lord the Legate to the lowest acolyte in his train, and I pledge my coat of mail (you know it, of Italian workmanship and inlaid with silver and ivory) you will come off with safety and honour."

"Honour!" repeated young Raymond bitterly. "God keep me from such honour! Can honour survive when mercy and truth are gone forever? Consider what you ask. Of my retainers – and faithful retainers have they been to me and mine – my lord knows that more than half abhor the Mass, and follow the Albigensian and Pateran heresies."

"Then let the slaves abjure their heresies and obey their lawful lords," said the Count of Toulouse. He spoke with angry impatience, for a consciousness of being in the wrong, which he tried hard to smother, irritated his naturally mild temper, and during the whole of their protracted interview he had been reasoning down his own better self, as well as the generous resolution of his youthful kinsman.

"They ought to," returned the Viscount, "but the question is, will they? You can answer that! What have you seen in your own territories since the Legate and his satellites have taken the power into their hands, and begun to 'make inquisition for heresy?'"

A change passed over his young eager face as he added, "And *I* have seen things of which I hardly dare to speak or *think*, lest I should doubt that there is a God in Heaven who sees them too. Tortures, murders, conflagrations, a fruitful land reduced to desolation. The infidel Saracen is a nobler foe than these Crusaders, with the white cross on their arms and every evil passion in their hearts. At least, the infidel fights with *men*, but the Crusader wreaks his direst vengeance on the innocent and helpless – on womanhood, which every true knight should protect at the expense of his heart's best blood – on childhood, which appeals, with the strong cry of its weakness, to all that is human within us. Did they not burn…"

"It is useless to dwell on atrocities that we all lament," the Count interrupted uneasily.

"But it is not useless to prevent them in future. This much at least I say: before they do such things in the lands of Beziers, the lord of Beziers will sacrifice his life."

"Foolish boy! What do you wish to do? Can you scrape together, out of all your lands of Beziers and Albi, so many as eight or ten thousand men? Yet you talk as if you dreamed of taking the field against a host of three hundred thousand, headed by such chiefs as the Duke of Burgundy and the terrible De Montfort."

"I must defend my people," said the Viscount of Beziers.

"Defend them! That is clearly impossible. Will you perish with them, or will you save yourself while it is still possible?"

Raymond looked steadily in his uncle's face. His own was very pale, but his voice was firm and calm as he answered, "I will perish with them."

"If you are mad, I am not. The last counsel you shall ever have from my lips I give you now. Leave this place without an hour's delay, lest I find you quarters in the keep until your submission is lodged with our lord the Legate, and a branch of our ancient house saved from utter ruin."

"My lord!" exclaimed Raymond in a tone of indignant surprise.

"Go. Do not tempt me too far."

"It is indeed time that I should go, if it is thus the Count of Toulouse honours the ties of blood and friendship, and the solemn bond of a contract he cannot have forgotten."

"Do you dare to speak of that contract?" said the angry Count. "It is *you* who have forgotten. Could the madman who rushes on to certain ruin dream of claiming the alliance, the hand of…"

"Forbear, my lord; at least let that name not be named between us," said the youth in a tone of deep emotion, and he turned away his face. A moment afterward he resumed more calmly, "I must defend the cause of the oppressed. If I fall, I shall at least fall not dishonourably; you need not blush for me. And perhaps when the struggle – the unequal struggle – is over, and the last Viscount of Beziers has died for his people and his rights, Count Raymond of Toulouse may speak of his fate in other terms than he does now, and with a different feeling. Farewell!"

He turned to go, but when he had almost reached the door he looked back for a moment, and added, "My lord Count, the devil does not always keep his promises. Neither do the priests theirs. The security and peace for which you are bartering your conscience may not after all be yours. God grant you do not regret, when regrets are unavailing, that you did not act a nobler part."

He strode from the hall, and his angry, yet in heart half-relenting, kinsman soon heard his voice in the courtyard hastily summoning a favourite page, the only attendant he had brought with him on his rapid and secret journey.

The Count of Toulouse and Raymond de Beziers met no more on earth. The former went to Rome, to seal his disgraceful peace with the persecuting power which was carrying fire and sword into the heart of his fair dominions, and dooming his innocent vassals to a thousand torturing forms of death. The latter, despairing but resolved, took his homeward way with these words on his lips: "I will die with my people!"

So their paths divided.

II

The Page's Story

THE YOUNG KNIGHT and his attendant rode
on in silence amid the vineyards and the ol-
iveyards of fair Languedoc. War (that worst
of all wars, kindled by fanaticism) had not yet
laid its blighting hand on the district through
which they passed, and all looked bright and
pleasant in the sunshine of early spring. But in

Raymond's soul there was darkness. He had believed it possible, by an effort of heroic courage, and with the assistance and hearty cooperation of the Count of Toulouse, to turn back the tide of the crusading army, and for this time at least to save his people; but the defection of his powerful kinsman changed the aspect of affairs. Already the cause had become desperate. Now it seemed utterly hopeless, yet with a clear apprehension of the danger, and a resolute though breaking heart, he chose to die rather than abandon it, for he could not desert his vassals, and consent to witness and abet the cruelties of the Crusade and the Inquisition. Still life had high hopes for him. One hope especially there was, closely entwined with the friendship and favour of the Count of Toulouse, with which it was hard to part – how hard might perhaps be revealed by the mute anguish of his gaze as he turned it on the lofty battlements of the castle, before the winding road concealed them from his view. Then there passed over his face a look of stern, almost defiant resolution; he was arming himself with the courage of despair, but it was armour that tortured while it strengthened – a cuirass worn above a recent wound.

After riding along for some time at a rapid pace, he checked his steed a little, and called, "Henri!"

The page spurred his stout palfrey to the side of his master's horse, and raised his large dark eyes, full of the fire and softness of a southern clime. The boy was of noble birth; it is well known that the office, which his close-fitting jerkin of fine cloth and plumed cap betokened, was considered in that age the most fitting preparation for the duties of knighthood. He looked sad and thoughtful— remarkably so for one so young, but this might have arisen from his evident though silent sympathy with the sorrow of his lord. Ignorant of the business which had brought them to Toulouse, the page formed his own conjectures. Among the retainers of both houses rumors were rife of the proposed alliance between the young Viscount of Beziers and the beautiful and only daughter of Count Raymond VI of Toulouse. When, therefore, the Viscount left his uncle's castle hastily, without ceremony and with a frown on his brow, when no admission was vouchsafed him to the "bower" where the Lady Beatrice and her attendants told their beads, wrought marvelous embroidery, and listened to the *chanzos* and *sirventes* of the troubadors, what could an observant page who loved his master conclude, save that some terrible obstacle— probably a quarrel between the uncle and nephew— had unexpectedly arisen? He was thinking very hardly of the Count, upon whom he of course laid the entire blame, when his lord's voice called him to his side.

"Henri de la Vaur," said he, "thou halt never told me thy history. I know it from others, but would fain hear it now from thine own lips."

"There is but little to tell, my noble lord," replied the boy sadly.

"Thou wert born amidst those grand white mountains yonder?" said the knight, pointing towards a faint white line near the horizon, where the distant Pyrenees might be rather dreamed than seen.

"No, my lord," answered the page. "I have been there with our kindred, at Minerbe, but I was born in our own castle of La Vaur. I scarce remember my father, the lord of La Vaur, he fell in battle more than ten years ago; but my mother, the Lady Girarde— ah, my lord has surely heard of her— she was so beautiful, so good. The poor all loved her, and from her gate was none ever sent empty away. Most gently she comforted those who were in sorrow; most tenderly she ministered to the sick; the orphans were to her as her own children;— she thought of all, cared for all."

Here the boy stopped abruptly, overcome by his emotion. The young Viscount's thoughts reverted to his own beautiful and brilliant mother, Adelaide of Toulouse, whose charms were sung by the most celebrated of the troubadors, in *chanzos* which still exist for the study of the antiquarian. How different from hers was the tranquil life of the Albigensian lady! Yet this had an austere and quiet loveliness, almost more captivating, he thought, than all the glare and glitter of the court beauty's triumphant career.

"I have heard of the good deeds of the Lady Girarde de la Vaur," he said compassionately. "No doubt they deserve the favor of God, and were not forgotten by Him."

Henri looked perplexed, and after some moments' thought, he answered modestly and in a low voice, "I am sure God has not forgotten them, my dear lord. But she always knew He loved her, and had forgiven her sins for the blessed Savior's sake. She did these things only because her heart thanked Him for His grace and love, and she longed so much to please Him. All her life was one great song of thankfulness, like those grand old hymns you sing in chapel, high and holy yet so sweet." He paused, but the Viscount said, "Go on, Henri."

"At last," he resumed, "there was a rumor of war in the land, and our people said to each other in terror that the Crusaders were coming. Our castle of La Vaur could not well be defended, and we had but few fighting men amongst our retainers, but my mother's brother, the noble Lord Almeric, a brave and skillful captain, came to our help, and encouraged us to do our best and hold out to the last. Our attendants also (who were all of our own faith save old Gaston the seneschal) were well armed and courageous, so it seemed best to us to put our trust in God and to strengthen our fortifications to stand a siege. Scarce had we finished this work when the Crusaders came. It may be we might have wearied them out, but alas! our supply of provisions failed! What could we do? My uncle and his knights deemed it wisest to surrender, making such terms as they could with the besiegers. Would to God they had said like King David, 'better to fall into the hands of the Lord God than into the hands of man!'

"That fatal morning, when the castle gates were thrown open to our enemies, my mother and I sat alone in our apartment. Defense and flight were alike impossible, and as it was thought best to avoid all show of attempting either, she would not allow even our personal attendants to gather round us. We clung close together, listening to the cries and the tumult outside, and for a long time we did not speak.

"At last she said, 'Let us pray to God.' She knelt and prayed, 'O God our Father, strengthen us to witness for Thy name, and if it be Thy will, take us quickly home to Thee, through the merits of our Savior Christ.' Then she rose and stood beside me, looking very pale but calm. I still knelt, she laid her hand on my head and said in a firm voice. 'My son, promise thy mother thou wilt never deny the Lord thy Savior.'

"I answered, 'Mother, I promise'; and she bent down and kissed my brow, a long burning kiss,— I feel it still,— it was her last." He paused for a few moments and then continued with at least outward calmness, "I know not how long it was ere the door was rudely thrust open, and some six or seven fierce-looking Crusaders rushed in, the foremost had an ax in his hand, there was blood upon it, and I mind me the white cross on his arm was streaked with blood.

"'Yield, heretics!' he cried, brandishing his weapon.

"My mother said, 'We yield, only lead us without violence to your general.' The wretch sprang forward and seized her arm as if to drag her with them. I threw myself on him and struck him with all my might."

"Bravely done, boy! Well?"

"He raised his axe. The room seemed to fall on me. I knew no more. When I regained consciousness it was night, the moonlight lay on the floor in long, narrow streaks. I was alone. The only thought that found place in my mind was this one, 'Where is my mother?' I tried to stand, but felt strangely weak and faint, and putting my hand on the floor beside me found it was wet with blood.

"At last I managed to rise, and with great difficulty succeeded in clambering up to the high narrow window, which looked out on the courtyard. What a sight met my eyes! All below me looked black in the moonlight— frightfully black! Fragments of wood and other rubbish half consumed by fire covered the ground— and amongst them, gleaming hideously, white, there were— there were—"

"Of what horrors dost thou speak?" cried Raymond.

"My lord," returned the page, "in that court-yard they burned to death, in one great fire, more than a hundred men and women. Besides these were eighty persons hanged on lofty gibbets, among them my noble Uncle Almeric. 'Shall I not visit for these things, saith the Lord?" and the boy's breast heaved, and his slight form seemed to dilate with the passion that filled his soul.

"Better to cast in my lot with thee than with them," said the young Viscount thoughtfully to himself. He added aloud, "But thy lady mother, what of her?"

"Not *there,* my lord," said the page.

"A vague, nameless, horrible dread came over me at what I beheld. I tried to cry aloud, but something choked my voice, and letting go my hold of the window, I fell to the ground and again lost consciousness. How long I lay thus I know not, but it was still night when I felt some one touch me, and heard old Gaston's voice. I whispered, 'Gaston, tell me in pity where is my mother, does she live?'

"His answer was, 'She lives, come with me, I will take you to her.' God forgive him! but the lie saved my life, for the hope it brought me sent new strength through my feeble limbs. He bound my wound, gave me a draft of water, threw a cloak round my shoulders, and led me through the long passages to a small private door of the castle. There a man, also wrapped in a cloak, stood waiting with two horses. Gaston exchanged a few words with him too low for me to hear, and put something into his hand. Then we mounted, and as Gaston did so, I saw in the moonlight that he wore the hateful white cross. When the sentries challenged us, he gave them the pass-word of the night ('The wounds of St. Sebastian,' I think it was) so we rode away safely, and being mercifully preserved through many dangers, at last we reached your town of Beziers, where my noble lord so kindly and generously took us under his protection."

"But how could Gaston induce one of those pitiless wretches to aid your escape?" asked the Viscount.

"By discovering to him the place where my mother had concealed her jewels," answered Henri. "My lord knows that Gaston, himself a Catholic, ought to have been in no danger; but they were so fierce and cruel that he would have been dragged to death in spite, as he hath it, 'of all the blessed saints in paradise,' as well as of his own earnest protestations that he was neither an Albigense nor a Pateran, nor of any sect whatever, had not a captain, under whom he once served against the Moors in Spain, rescued him from the fury of his soldiers. And then he witnessed all, *all* the fearful scene. He stood near my dear mother when she answered for her faith and chose death rather than life at the price of forsaking her Savior. Oh, why was I not there? Why did God deny me the grace to die with her?"

"Because thou wert too young to die, poor child," said his master kindly.

"Oh, no, my lord; boys younger than I have died ere this for the name of Christ. They allowed Gaston to come near enough to speak with her. She said God was with her, and she was not afraid. Then she added low. 'Remember the charge I gave thee.' That charge was to save me. She put into his hand for me a string of pearls that she always wore round her neck, and a little book more precious than pearls or gold. Then they led her away to death. Gaston kept beside her to the last, and saw the end. She was stoned." But the boy's voice was choked by emotion, and he was unable to proceed.

"Henri de la Vaur," said the Viscount in a tone of deep feeling, "God helping me, I will sheathe my sword in the hearts of these miscreants. I swear it."

The page looked up in surprise. "My lord will not, cannot fight with the Crusaders?"

"I must do that thing," returned Raymond, "or give up thee, my child, and all the men women and children who hold thy faith, to be dealt with as were the people of La Vaur. I have heard enough, boy. Thou hast given me what I needed— a thought to nerve my arm in the conflict and to make my heart hard and wild with vengeance, as it should be for such a struggle."

Then there was silence again between the knight and his attendant, and the page dropped once more into his place behind; and as he did so he murmured to himself, "'And Jesus said, Father, forgive them, for they know not what they do.' Merciful Savior, teach him in Thine own time and in Thine own way."

III

"The Holy War"

Some months elapsed since the Count of Toulouse and the Viscount of Beziers parted in wrath and forever. The young Viscount spent the greater part of them in preparations for a heroic struggle against overwhelming odds. Leaving his capital town of Beziers in the care of his lieutenants, he shut himself up in Carcassone, determining to await the enemy there, and prolong his resistance to the last. But in the month of June horrible tidings reached him, which wrung, though they could not shake, his steadfast heart. The Crusaders had taken Beziers by assault, and put all who were found within its walls, to the number of sixty thousand, to the sword, without distinction of age, of sex or of creed. When the ferocious Arnaud, abbot of the Cistercians, was reminded that there were many good Catholics in the town, and asked by what means might they be distinguished from the heretics, his answer was, "Kill them all; God will know who belong to Him." And the hideous command was fulfilled to the letter.

A few strong and simple words from a contemporary Provencal historian, himself a Roman Catholic, give a striking picture of the scene:— "They entered the city of Beziers, where they murdered more people than was ever known in the world; for they spared neither young nor old, nor infants at the breast. They killed and murdered them all, which being seen by the said people of the city they that were able did retreat into the great church of St. Nazarius, both men and women. The chaplains thereof, when they retreated, caused the bells to ring until everybody was dead; but neither the sound of the bells, nor the chaplains in their priestly habits, nor the clerks, could hinder all from being put to the sword. Only one escaped, for all the rest were slain and died. Nothing so pitiable was ever heard of or done. And when the city had been pillaged, it was set on fire; so that it was all pillaged and burnt, as it appears to this day. No living thing was left, which was a cruel vengeance, seeing that the said Viscount was neither a heretic, nor of their sect."

After this frightful event, the whole strength of the crusading army, numbering about three hundred thousand men, was turned against

Carcassone. For some time Raymond held out, like a wild boar brought to bay by its pursuers—despairing yet dauntless. At length there shone upon his arms one of those transient flickers of success that sometimes light a dying cause. Despair is strong and more than once or twice the sallies of the brave garrison spread dismay through the mighty host whose tents lay white upon all the surrounding plain.

The chiefs of that host—the Duke of Burgundy and the Count of Nevers—as well as the crafty Legate and the fierce De Montfort—began to allow to each other that this young Viscount of Beziers was no contemptible adversary. Whispers of a possible accommodation began to be heard, and the more readily since such a measure need cost the Crusaders but little, the views of Rome upon the necessity of keeping faith with heretics being proverbially lax. Time was precious, and pledges and promises were easily given.

Besides all this, the King of Arragon, Pedro II, who accompanied the crusading army, was a friend and relative of the Viscount, and now showed a disposition to interfere on his behalf. He actually procured an interview with him, and returned to the camp deeply impressed by his gallant and generous spirit, and the manly eloquence with which he maintained the righteousness of his cause.

But the Legate turned a deaf ear to his warm intercessions, and the only grace which the priests who governed the army would offer the people of Carcassone was a permission for thirteen of their number, including the Viscount, to leave the city— the remainder to expect the fate of the people of Beziers. History has preserved Raymond's answer to this proposal. "I would consent," said he, "to be flayed alive, rather than abandon a single one of my fellow-citizens." And "he persisted in defending himself with unconquerable valor."

But renewed offers of accommodation were made; the Crusaders lowered their tone, and seemed to become far less insolent and over-bearing. "If the Legate and the Viscount could only meet," they said, "they would be able mutually to satisfy each other, and all would be well."

Finally, the Legate sent an officer of rank into Carcassone, to urge this proposal upon the Viscount, offering him a full safe-conduct for himself and his attendants, secured by the most solemn oaths. Raymond, after much deliberation, agreed to visit the camp, probably considering that the presence of the friendly and powerful King of Arragon was a sufficient guarantee against any meditated treachery.

Early in the morning on the day appointed for the Viscount's interview, the Legate, arrayed in a sort of knightly deshabille, sat before a small table at the upper end of a large hall. Piles of lances and other weapons occupied the lower part, pieces of armor were scattered around, and soldiers, citizens, and servants passed to and fro. Upon the table lay his own morion and steel gloves, and a very beautiful sword with a jeweled hilt and scabbard, while a flask of rare wine and some coarse black bread contrasted with these and with each other.

The young champion of the Albigenses sat buried in profound thought, his head resting on both hands, and his face concealed from view. It was not without counting the cost that he had taken up arms for that persecuted people. From boyhood his mind had been exercised upon the problem of their infidelity, heresy, or *faith*, as he had learned at last to call it. The necessity, early imposed on him, of thinking and acting for himself, gave stability and self-reliance to his character, whilst the existence of a numerous body of men among his vassals who, like himself, were of a reasoning and reflective cast of mind, contributed to stimulate these faculties to still more effective exercise. And now that the crisis had arrived, and that he went forth to plead the cause of his people before a judge that he well knew to be both perfidious and relentless, he was gravely weighing all the probabilities of the case. Notwithstanding his precautions, he might be the victim of some secret snare, he and the band of gallant men, his best and bravest, whom he deemed it his wisest course to take with him. What if they never returned to Carcassone? Should he draw them too into this peril? Yes—if he played his game, it behooved him to play it fearlessly. Mercy and truth might yet be found in yonder camp, and fair terms be obtained for his vassals. Of his own life he scarcely thought; except as involving the one great question of their deliverance, he regarded it with mournful, even with bitter indifference. But was it well to die in conflict with holy Mother Church? Who would raise the crucifix before his eyes, and touch his cold forehead with the sacred oil? He must not, however, in this his hour of action, lose himself again in that sea of confused contradictory thought. God's law and the Church's law being as he believed in conflict, he chose to abide on God's side and to take the consequences.

"Oh, all-merciful!" was the cry that arose from his heart, "to Thee I appeal. Stand by me while I strive for mercy and truth— stand by me if I fall in that sacred cause. I ask it in the name of Thy Son, the ever-merciful." He raised his head slowly, and saw his page, Henri de la Vaur, beside him.

"My lord," said the boy, "the good father Sicard waits without."

"Let him enter," returned the Viscount. "I sent for him."

Henri ushered in a venerable man with gray hair and beard, in plain dark attire. He bowed to the Viscount and stood in silence, awaiting his pleasure.

"Well, Barbe," said Raymond, "what news?"

"None, my lord, save that our people pray day and night that He who keepeth Israel may keep you beneath the shadow of His wings."

"Dost thou hear them murmur at our strict economy of food?"

"Nay, Viscount, it would ill beseem them.

Life could be sustained on far less than we consume, and were it otherwise, every man, woman, and child, among us would perish with hunger rather than open our gates to the enemy!"

"Brave words, Barbe, and not spoken at random either. Now hearken. I go forth today to make terms, if so it may be, not for myself, but for thee and thy people. I pledge my knightly word that neither threat nor promise shall sever my fate from theirs and thine. Dost thou trust me?"

"I do, so help me God!" said the old pastor

with deep feeling. "May He reward thee, and He surely will."

A look of emotion passed over Raymond's face. "Thy people have ever dealt well with me and mine," he said, stretching out his hand.

Father Sicard took it and raised it to his lips, while he said with great earnestness, "Would that my good lord could say, 'Thy people shall be my people, and thy God my God.' Would that he knew that precious faith which can keep the heart at peace in the midst of peril, suffering, death itself— that he knew *Him* who is at once the author of that faith and its objects,— then indeed the worst that could come, would but change his coronet into a crown of glory, that would shine forever and ever."

The Viscount was silent and turned away his face, but the page Henri unconsciously drew closer, and fixed his large dark eyes, first on the speaker, then on his beloved young master with an expression of earnest entreaty.

At last Raymond said, with a smile and rather lightly, "So thou wouldst make me a heretic, Sicard. 'Twere more to the purpose if thou and thy brethren would return to the true Church, and save much blood and many tears."

But the last words were spoken gravely, and a sad and thoughtful look replaced the smile.

"Barbe," he added after a pause, "I summoned thee as a man of sense and intelligence, and one respected by thine own people. I have a secret to confide to thee Henri, fetch hither a lantern."

The boy obeyed. Raymond took it from his hand and led away the pastor, forbidding Henri by a gesture to follow them. A considerable time elapsed before he returned, then he came alone, having dismissed Sicard.

Henri ventured to ask as he passed, "Is it my lord's pleasure that I should attend him to the camp?"

"No, my poor little heretic," returned the

Viscount kindly, "those wild Crusaders would matter little tearing thee to pieces in their zeal for mother Church, so should I lose the best page a knight ever had."

Something in the lord's manner, both to the Pastor Sicard and to himself, touched the boy deeply. "He never used," he thought, "to give his hand to one of our people, and then his words are so gentle— it seems like taking farewell of us." His face flushed, then grew pale again as he knelt quickly at the feet of his master. "A boon, my noble lord, a boon ere you leave us."

"Speak boldly, my child. God knows it is little I have to give, but thou art welcome to the best. What is it? A sword? A good steed?" Henri drew a strange-looking little volume from beneath his jerkin. It was clasped with gold, and the covers were curiously chased and adorned with the same precious metal. So small were its dimensions that it might have been worn, as such treasures have been, set in a brooch upon a lady's breast.

"Will my lord condescend to take this with him? It will do him good."

"Well, boy, if it please thee. Certainly it will do me no harm. I thank thee." And he took the little book in his hand and examined it curiously. "Hath it the virtue of a talisman, thinkest thou? Will it turn aside the brand or the lance in the day of battle? Or will it give me good success in the business upon which I now go forth?"

Henri rose up well pleased. "I do not know, my lord," he answered simply. "In truth I have never thought; but it does the *soul* good, for it tells of Jesus, the good Savior, who loves us.

"All these people's religion consists in a fervent faith in Christ, and a strong persuasion of His love to them," thought Raymond, "and that, it seems, is heresy. Passing strange!" He added aloud, "And now, Henri, take my sword *Joyeuse,* and make him as bright as thou canst. Time presses."

The next day there was bitter weeping and wailing in Carcassone. The brave young chieftain returned no more from that fatal camp, the dark abode of treachery and violence. Long did the townsfolk watch and wait, anxiously keeping hope alive in each other's hearts. But when the sun of the second day reached its meridian, and no message or token came from the camp, even the strongest-hearted felt they were abandoned to their fate.

The Albigenses would have been more than human had not a few voices been raised to accuse their absent lord of a faithless desertion of their cause. But the murmur was hushed at once. "He would never forsake us— never," said they all. "His heart is true as steel. But alas! by this time he does not live, or only lives a captive."

Then wilder and louder grew the voice of

weeping. The people of Carcassone seemed already to behold the swords of the Crusaders, red from the slaughter of Beziers, at their breasts. Husbands clasped their wives, and parents their children. "God help us, we must die!" they murmured in their despair. But from many hearts in that hour of anguish there arose the cry, "We are Thine, O Savior Christ— receive us!"

Above the sobbing and the praying of the crowd gathered in the market-place arose a calm clear voice, speaking hope.

"My children," said the Pastor Sicard, "do not abandon yourselves to despair. It is true that we cannot continue to defend the city, yet with God's good help, we may still be saved. Our noble Viscount, ere he left us, revealed to me the entrance to a secret passage, winding beneath the fortifications, and afterward underground till it reaches the castle you know of, three leagues on the right hand of our town.

Let us wait until the darkness of night makes it possible for our soldiers to leave the ramparts unobserved. Let us kneel once more in the church at the door of which I stand, and there commit ourselves to the merciful protection of Almighty God. Let us then escape thither, and thence we can go forth in His name, whithersoever He may please to lead us; for the whole earth is His, and the fullness thereof."

Eager murmurs amongst the crowd greeted the pastor's proposal. "God be praised. —He has not forsaken us!" was, the first thought of those humble and pious sufferers for their faith. And the foremost men among them added words like these: "Father Sicard is right; he is a good man, we will all follow him."

At the dark midnight hour the sorrowful 'remnant of the Albigenses set out on their perilous journey, taking with them provisions for three days, and in a few instances, such valuables as they could conceal about their person.

It was a silent melancholy procession. Mothers carried their infants in their arms, fathers led their little children by the hand. The sick and aged were borne by their friends, with all the care and tenderness that circumstances permitted; for suffering had not made these poor people hard and unfeeling towards each other.

Almost at the last moment Sicard missed Henri de la Vaur, who in the early part of the evening had made himself very useful. He remembered having seen him in the church, and hastening thither, found him still kneeling, his earnest face raised upwards and his hands clasped in prayer. He bade him in a tone of authority rise immediately and follow him.

Henri rose, but said very calmly, "I am praying for my master, and I wish to stay here until the Crusaders enter the town, that if he be a captive they may allow me to go to him and serve him."

"Nay, my son," replied the pastor; "it is a

foolish, though a brave and generous thought.

They would murder thee, or force thee perchance by torture to deny thy faith. It is wrong to *seek* such peril, though we should face it bravely when God sends it. Come."

But Henri still hung back "This delay may ruin us all," said Sicard sternly. "Yet I leave not this spot without thee; for," he added, "there is none in all the city whom he would rather save."

"I go, then, my father," said Henri; but he murmured in a low voice, "I shall see my dear lord yet, for all that"; and the boy's pale, resolved countenance struck the aged pastor. They both rejoined the band of fugitives, which immediately began its dreary march; and thus it happened that when the morning's sun rose in glory over the city, it shone upon deserted ramparts and empty houses. Not a living soul was left in Carcassone. Vainly had Raymond of Beziers been entreated to save himself, and leave the men of Carcassone to perish. He would not have it thus, therefore another lot was appointed him. *He* fell, but they were saved. And it was better so for him.

IV

Conclusion

The snow fell in Beziers, covering, with its spotless veil, as if in pity, the charred and blackened ruins, and the streets where so lately blood had flowed in rivers. All was desolation there, made only more dreary by the troops of rough and fierce Crusaders who trod the streets, and occupied such of the dwellings as the fire left habitable—dwellings which once were homes, but which were now more in common with the dens of wild beasts. For having killed, the spoilers also took possession. But little joy or profit did such possession bring. The arms of the "white cross host" only availed them to pull down and to destroy; their commission was not in any sense to restore or to rebuild.

The castle of Beziers shared the fate of the town. Plundered, dismantled, and partly destroyed by fire, the favorite residence of the young Viscount— where the proud Roger Taillefer held his court, and the Troubadors sang the praises of the beautiful Adelaide of Toulouse— was now only fit to be used as a prison. The cruel and perfidious De Montfort, whose services to the cause had been rewarded by a grant of the broad lands of the captive Viscount, set little value upon such a residence. Sufficient for his purpose if its gloomy walls were still strong enough to keep, not a crowd of ignoble heretics awaiting their doom, but some political prisoner of importance. The fierce-looking band of Crusaders who guarded it night and day seemed to indicate that it was being employed for such a purpose, especially as they wore, in addition to the white cross on their arms, the badge of the private retainers of De Montfort.

A bare-footed friar, habited in a coarse serge gown, and with his beads in his hand, passed out of the castle. The group of soldiers gathered round the entrance made way for him obsequiously, for he was no less a person than the celebrated Izarn, "Dominican missionary and inquisitor." He looked up from his rosary to mutter a benediction upon them. As he did so, his eye was caught by that of a man in a rich dress, who stood a little apart, conversing with a young lad, apparently a page or messenger from some chieftain of rank.

"Your blessing, holy father," said the captain, for such he was, uncovering his head. The friar drew near to him.

"The De Montfort has a faithful servant in you, captain," he observed in the *Langue d' Oc,* and with a keen glance that gave some sinister meaning to his words.

The soldier's eye fell; he seemed to relish the commendation but little. He asked hastily, and in the same language, "Does the prisoner become more docile to your pious instructions, father?"

"Never a whit," returned the friar angrily; "he is obstinate as any of that accursed race with whom he has allied himself." He added in a whisper, "And he will *die* un-reconciled to the Church."

"*Die,* father!" repeated the captain uneasily, changing his position.

The friar laid his hand on his arm.

"Come, we understand each other," he said.

"He is dying, captain. You best know how. Of a broken heart, *we shall say.*"

The captain raised his eye-brows, shrugged his shoulders, and remarked with a little hesitation, 'Yet is it a pity, father, were it not for the sake of Holy Church. So young, and of such noble lineage; gentle too, and courteous, and bearing himself throughout with most undaunted courage."

A sneer passed over the Dominican's hard face.

"It is full late," he said, "for *thee* to talk of pity, save to blind some idiot who knows no better. Thou dolt pity, as the hawk pities the sparrow!" He seemed about to turn away, then added aloud, "Who is that boy?"

"An old retainer of the prisoner's, father, who prays that he may go and minister to him. Believing it to be the will of Holy Church that all possible gentleness and mercy should be shown, I have given him permission. Forgive me, father, if I have erred in this." The good captain did not think it necessary to add that the young suppliant had enforced his entreaties by the gift of two large pearls of considerable value.

"Absolvo te," said the friar with a grim smile. "But is it *safe,* my friend? Such as he have oft-times sharp ears and long tongues. "I risk that," answered the soldier. "Easier to enter these walls than to quit them," and the friar passed on.

A few moments more, and Henri de la Vaur had obtained the desire of his heart, that for which he had braved many perils and endured many hardships. He stood once more in the presence of his lord the Viscount of Beziers. He stood in his presence, yet he saw him not. Mastering the rush of emotion which brought the tears to his eyes and drove the color from his cheek, he gazed around the dreary comfortless hall. The Viscount there, and neither to speak to him nor to call him to his side, there was something in this so strange that it chilled his heart. At last he saw the object of his search at one end of the room, reclining on a crude couch covered with a piece of tapestry which had been torn from the wall.

Another moment found him on his knees beside him, pressing his hand to his lips. "My dear master!" he murmured in a choking voice.

The once proud and fiery-hearted young knight opened his eyes languidly, and fixed them on him, but did not speak. His face was worn and pale, but its expression, though mournful, was calm and not unhappy; it told of past rather than of present suffering.

"Do you not remember me, my good lord!" said the boy.

"Henri? Yes," Raymond answered softly. "Yes, my child, I remember thee. But old faces come to me, so often now, as I lie here betwixt sleep and waking, that I doubt if this be not also a dream."

Worn out by anxiety and by toil, the boy could restrain his tears no longer. Hiding his face in the tapestry of the couch, he wept and sobbed aloud for some minutes. He feared this was the worst thing he could have done; but it proved the best, for it roused the dying man from his torpor.

Half raising himself, Raymond laid his wasted hand on the boy's head, saying gently, "Poor child, do not weep. More help and comfort than thou canst know have come to me in these dark hours. Look here," and with his other hand he sought for something on the couch. It was soon found, and light flashed through Henri's tears as he recognized his own gift— his mother's little book, the Gospel of St. John.

"But by what strange chance art thou here?" asked the Viscount, with something like a return of his natural animation of manner. "Art thou also a prisoner?"

"I came of my own free will to seek my good and kind lord, and to share his fortunes," answered Henri.

Raymond's large languid eyes filled with tears. He did not speak, but raising himself with much difficulty he drew the boy towards him and embraced him. "Brave and faithful child," he murmured at last, "thou dost love on still, when the rest— I deemed myself forgotten by all the world."

Henri knew how to strike a chord sure to respond to his touch. "My lord," he said, "the remnant escaped from Carcassone are safe and trust to make good their retreat to another land."

Raymond's features brightened. "Thank God! then all has not been in vain. Hath any man assumed the command amongst them?"

"Yes, my lord; they all consent to obey the good Pastor Sicard."

"It is well. Where one man knows to command, and the rest obey, there is hope. Thou didst leave Carcassone in their company then?"

"But with the settled purpose of quitting them, and returning to you as speedily as I might."

"Did they know this purpose of thine?"

"I dreamed of stealing away in secret lest they should hinder me. But this plan seemed ungrateful to Sicard, who loved me as a father. So I confided all to him."

"And he tried to dissuade thee, I warrant."

"Well, at first he feared I should never succeed in reaching your— the place where you were."

"My *prison,*" said Raymond, with a smile of resignation, more sad than Henri's tears.

"But when I told my plan, and explained how I would bribe the soldiers to give me what I wanted, he yielded, and blessed me and prayed God I might prosper. And then the people came round me, and I think they would have had me take all the gold and jewels they had amongst them; and some wanted to go with me, but that would only have been more danger and no help, for the soldiers do not care for a boy like me so much as for a grown man, and even the monks think I am the servant of some lord or knight, and not an Albigense or a heretic. As for the gold, they pressed it upon me so much that I took a few marks to pay my charges by the way, but for gaining my will from these Crusaders I have what is better than gold." And he cautiously drew from beneath his jerkin what had been a string of fine pearls, but the string was broken, and more than half the pearls were gone.

"Thou hast given all for me, poor child," said Raymond.

"And has not my good lord given all for me and mine?" answered the boy through his tears. "Our people would have sacrificed their lives to serve you," he added. "Words cannot tell how they mourned for you."

"May God preserve and prosper them," returned Raymond. "As for thee, my child, it is good to have thee with me, and to know that a friendly hand will close my eyes. Do not grieve that my hours are numbered. My captivity has not been so sweet that I should greatly regret its close. And this must have come sooner or later. The De Montfort could never have enjoyed his domains in peace whilst Raymond Roger de Beziers lived."

"It is he then who hath done this thing!" said Henri, starting.

"Be calm, my child," answered Raymond, gently. "Thou seest I am calm. Thy Book hath taught me, 'In my Father's house are many mansions'"; and he looked upwards, his face lighted with a beautiful expression of hope and confidence.

"You have found the Savior then," said

Henri, his own heart raised and awed into a calmness like that of the sufferer.

"I think He hath found me," was the low reply, and he murmured half to himself, "Jesus heard that they had cast him out, and —*He found him*— the words are in thy Book." He paused from exhaustion, and pointed to the table. Some wine lay upon it, which Henri brought, but he refused it, and asked for water, saying, "Beware of that wine, Henri— taste it not, touch it not, it would harm thee" —words which Henri did not fully comprehend until long afterward. After a short rest, he continued, "When first they led me here, a captive, I earnestly prayed that I might receive the holy rites of the Church. Upon one condition alone would the priests grant my prayer. I must acknowledge my sin in having resisted their arms."

"And that you would never do, my lord."

"Could I come before Him who is the

truth with a lie on my lips? Purchase the right to partake of His holy sacrament by a frightful sin? God forbid!— They declared me a heretic, excommunicated. Henri, thou canst not tell how it was with me then. All my life I had leant upon the Church, trusted in her aid, and now she forsook me, and I found myself alone, a naked soul trembling in the presence of my God, with death beside me, and all the sins of my youth rising up before my face. Men have never called me coward, yet I own that then I shivered in intolerable dread. Once it crossed my mind that since the Crusader believes that if he fell in battle with the Albigense, the gates of paradise would open before him and all his sins be blotted out, my conflict for truth and right might also be accepted by a righteous God. But I felt the thought an unutterable absurdity. As if I should say, 'Behold, I have, misspent my life, but I have given it at last in Thy cause,' — would He accept it at my hands? There was no help for me there— anywhere. At last I turned to thy Book, for I said, 'Let me read of Him with whom I have to do, that I may know if a man dare to hope in His mercy.' And then I read of the blessed Savior,— with strange, glad surprise I learned that He is no awful Judge, but the merciful and loving One, the Lamb of God who beareth away the sin the sin of the world— and mine. Alas, my strength fails, I cannot tell thee all."

He had told enough, however, to fill the simple heart of Henri with gratitude and joy. "It is well with me now," he continued. "He hath said, 'Peace I leave with you, my peace I give unto you,' and He is truth. Not one good word that He has spoken hath failed or shall fail in the last hour. They will say I died of a broken heart, but thou dost know better, my Henri."

"I do, and I will tell the truth," burst impetuously from Henri's lips.

"Nay, my child, I charge thee, as thou lovest me, seal thy lips until thou art safe beyond their power. A word, a look of suspicion, would be thy death-warrant. If thou canst, rejoin thine own people, the fugitives of Carcassone, and may God give thee rest, and deal kindly with thee as thou hast dealt with me."

"Hath my lord no parting word, no message for friend or relative?" asked Henri in a broken voice.

Some thought of long ago stirred the heart of the dying youth, and brought a faint glow to his pale cheek. Yet so long did the silence continue, that the page began to fear his question had been misunderstood. But it was not so. Raymond was wrestling with the last and strongest of earth's passions, and gathering power to put it calmly aside. At length he said, "I have no message, no relative survives who will mourn me. Yet didst thou chance to know, I should be glad to learn aught of my kinsman, the Count of Toulouse."

"Of the Count," returned Henri, "I have heard nothing special, nor yet of his son, but "Well?" said Raymond, observing his hesitation.

"At an inn where I stopped on my way thither, I conversed with a knight who had been in the train of the Lady Beatrice." Raymond heard the name with greater apparent calmness than Henri pronounced it, only a slight quiver passed over his face. "They have brought her to a convent in Spain for safety during these troublous times. The knight said the war and its consequences had affected her deeply."

"She is safe then, and at peace," said Raymond. "In everything God has cared for me. I had once a wild, foolish longing to send a token—"

"My lord, I would cross the world to do your pleasure, only tell me."

'No— no— better as it is. It might wake

sad memories, and I would not have one moment's pain given for me. I have done with these thoughts now. There is One I cannot love too well. I will think of Him."

There was a long silence, then Raymond asked feebly, "Is not the sun setting, Henri?" And in truth the rich red light, which told that the short winter's day had reached its close, stole across the couch, illuminating the form of the dying man and that of the young watcher by his side.

"Let in more light," said Raymond, "I have ever loved the light."

Henri went to the casement, and drew aside a piece of tapestry which partially served as a curtain. A flood of light filled the room immediately, and as the boy looked out on the gorgeous array of gold and purple clouds, he thought of the New Jerusalem, "having the glory of God, and her light like unto a stone most precious, even like a jasper stone, clear as crystal."

He said, returning to the couch, "My dear master will soon behold that land which has no need of the sun to shine in it, for 'the Lamb is the light thereof.' What glory that will be!"

"It may be so," answered Raymond, "but I want no glory, save to see His face. He loves me, He will receive me, that is all I know, and all I need." After a pause he added, "Now I am weary, I long to sleep." In a short time he slept (if indeed it was not rather a sort of stupor than a sleep) while Henri watched and wept silently by him during the long hours of darkness.

The next morning brought the zealous Izarn, eager to try once more the effect of his eloquence. But the ear of Raymond was closed to every voice save one,— that one which said, "Inasmuch as you have done it unto one of the least of these my brethren, you have done it unto Me."

For at midnight there came an angel of the

Lord, who opened the prison door and set the captive free. The angel's name was Death.

About the Author

DEBORAH ALCOCK (1835-1913) was a prolific Victorian author of historical fiction on religious themes. She was born in Ireland, where her father, the Venerable John Alcock, became Archdeacon of Waterford. She also wrote *The Czar* (1882), *Under the Southern Cross: Tales of the New World* (1900), and *Under Calvin's Spell* (1902).

About the Cántaro Institute
Inheriting, Informing, Inspiring

The Cántaro Institute is a confessional evangelical Christian organization established in 2020 that seeks to recover the riches of historic Protestantism for the renewal and edification of the contemporary church and to advance the comprehensive Christian philosophy of life for the religious reformation of the Western and Ibero-American world.

We believe that as the Christian church returns to the fount of Scripture as her ultimate authority for all knowing and living, and wisely applies God's truth to every aspect of life, faithful in spirit to the reformers, her missiological activity will result in not only the renewal of the human person but also the reformation of culture, an inevitable result when the true scope and nature of the gospel is made known and applied.

The Spanish Brothers is an accurate historical record of the rise, progress and fall of the Protestant Church in Spain. In particular, it mentions the history of the two great *Autos-de-fé* (Acts of faith: march and execution of the "heretics") in Seville. The only fictitious narrative enclosed is what corresponds to the personal history of the two brothers and their families. This masterful literary rendition portrays with excellence the biblical truth that God rewards His faithful servants up to a hundred times more, even in this life, for everything they do and suffer *por amor a su Nombre* — for the love of His Name.

This is the epic Cid, who in the last quarter of the eleventh century was banished by Alphonso VI of Castile, fought his way to the Mediterranean, stormed Valencia, married his two daughters to the Heirs of Carrión and defended his fair name in parliament and in battle. Here in this national epic, we see not only El Cid the militaristic hero, but also the loyal subject, the man of faith, the loving father, in truth, aspects of his character that many do not see or care to pay enough attention to. Behold, the Christian hero who was pivotal to the *Reconquista*, recovering Christian lands lost to invading Islamic forces.

www.ingramcontent.com/pod-product-compliance
Lightning Source LLC
Chambersburg PA
CBHW051234210726
48290CB00003B/963